Color THE ANCIENT FOREST

About The Wilderness Society

Since 1935, The Wilderness Society has been the leading national conservation organization working to protect America's wild lands and wildlife. More than 90 million acres of wilderness have been permanently protected through the organization's efforts. The Wilderness Society's expert staff of scientists, lawyers, lobbyists and journalists work in the nation's capital and in 16 regional offices to safeguard America's legacy of natural resources. The group is supported by more than 400,000 members nationwide. In 1991, the Society's top priority is saving the ancient forests of the Pacific Northwest.

LIVING PLANET
P R E S S

Author and illustrator: Ptolemy Tompkins
Cover Design and illustration: William Whitehead
Typography: Berna Alvarado-Rodriguez

Printed on recycled paper.

INTRODUCTION

How old is the house or apartment building you live in? Is it new or was it built many years ago? How old are the other buildings in your neighborhood? Twenty, 100, maybe 200 years old?

Now imagine a neighborhood as old as time. Imagine forests that stood when our ancestors lived in caves. The ancient forests of the Pacific Northwest have been growing for thousands of years, and some of the trees there are hundreds of years old. Today, you can reach out and touch the bark of a tree that an Indian hunter slept next to before Columbus arrived. But these ancient forests are more than just old trees. They include plants, birds, fish and many other kinds of animals. Even after they die, trees are homes to creatures like owls, woodpeckers and bears.

If you're lucky enough to visit one of these super-old forests, the first thing you'll notice is how BIG everything is. Look down at the soft carpet of fir needles that spreads out beneath the ancient branches. You might find a pinecone as big as a football. Gaze up into the branches that sway in the wind, and you might see a flying squirrel perched as high as a ten-story building.

The trees, plants and animals shown in this book all come from the western United States and Canada. Once, these forests grew throughout much of North America. Today, most of them are gone.

Every year, more of the ancient forest disappears. Trees are cut down for the wood to build houses, make furniture, paper and many other things. But if we keep cutting down trees in the ancient forests to get our wood, the forests as old as time will disappear forever. Instead, we could get our wood from younger trees, use less wood and recycle paper to help save our oldest forests.

The ancient forests need our help. As you read and color this book, you'll see why very old forests are so important. After all, without these trees there would be no forests for animals to live in or for people to visit when we want to remember just how old living things can be.

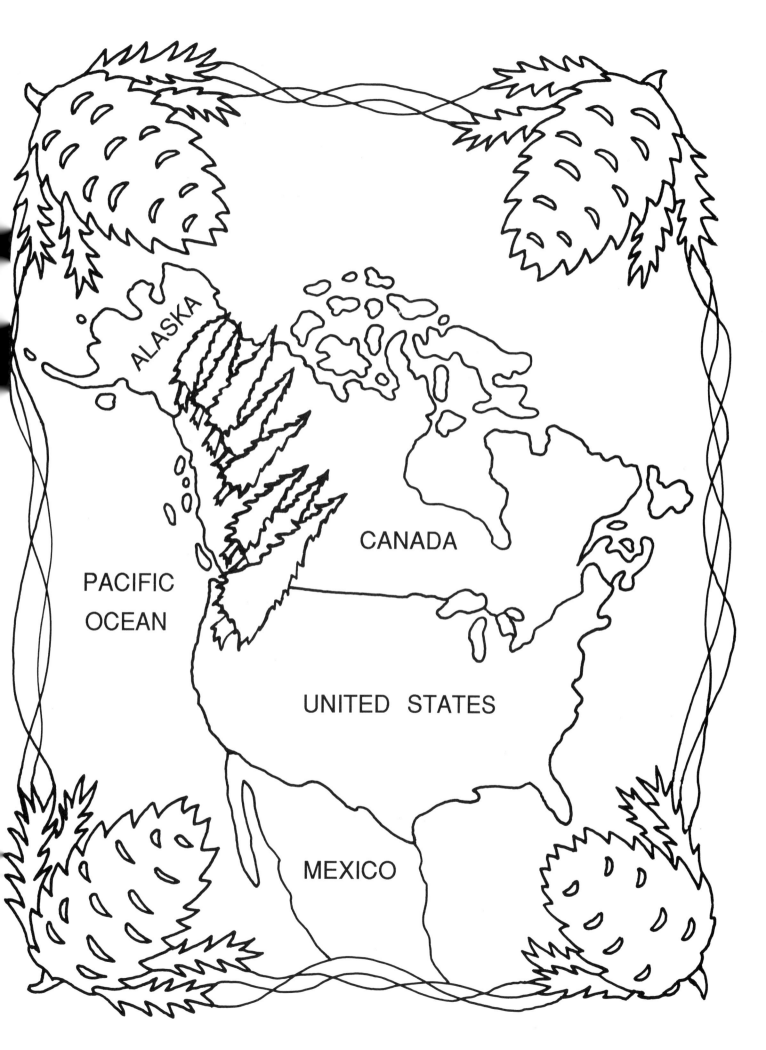

BLACK-TAILED DEER

A black-tailed deer wanders along the bank of a stream in search of berries. Black-tailed deer are smaller than other kinds of deer and their tails aren't really black. They are mostly white. Every summer, black-tailed deer grow antlers that drop off every winter.

SPOTTED OWL

Perched on the branch
of a hemlock tree,
a spotted owl scans the forest
with super-sensitive eyes.
All kinds of animals like to
live in the ancient forest,
but the spotted owl cannot
survive anywhere else.

BLACK BEAR

A mother black bear and her cub relax in a pool of sunlight. When a black bear spots a bees' nest in the branches of a tree, the bear might climb up to get some honey. This can be difficult since black bears can grow to be as tall as a full-grown man and weigh up to 500 pounds!

GOSHAWK

A goshawk rises from the forest floor on long, powerful wings and heads for its nest at the top of a dead fir tree. Like the owls that swoop and glide around the forest at night, the goshawk is a bird of prey. Birds of prey need to hunt other animals to stay alive.

RED TREE VOLE

A red tree vole nestles in
the prickly branches of a
Douglas fir. Voles eat
the tree's needles when
they're hungry and
lick the dew from them
when they're thirsty.
A vole can live its whole life
in a single tree!

TAILED FROG

A tailed frog passes a patch
of King Bolete mushrooms on
the way to the brook's edge.
Unlike other frogs, this
resident of the ancient forest
has a tail all its life.
The tailed frog likes the
brooks and still-water pools
that keep its body moist
and comfortable.

BOBCAT

The bobcat pads silently through the ancient forest in search of rabbits. Big, bright yellow eyes suit the bobcat well, since its day begins when the sun sets and the forest floor grows dark and quiet.

PILEATED WOODPECKER

Tap! Tap! Tap!
A pileated woodpecker drills a hole in a dead tree to search for ants. When a tree dies in the ancient forest, it often stays standing for years. Trees like this are called *snags*. Many animals make their homes in them. A snag is the woodpecker's favorite place to find a meal.

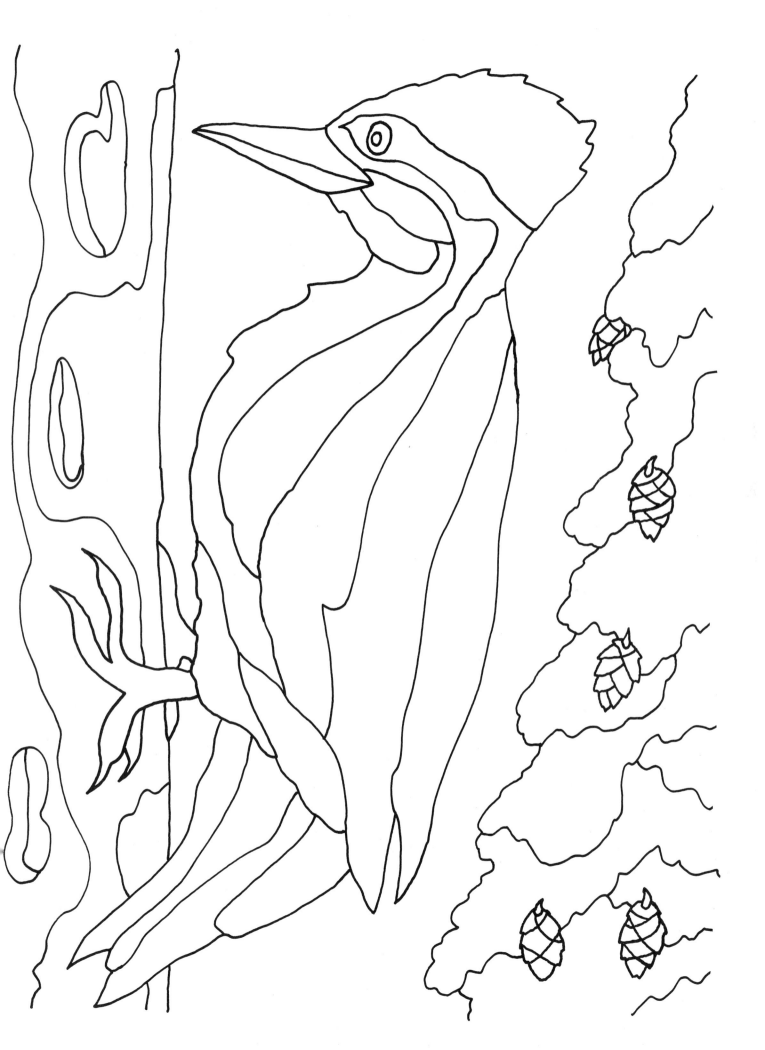

FLYING SQUIRREL

A family of flying squirrels climbs out of its nest in a hollow tree and glides off in search of food. Flying squirrels don't really fly. They jump from high up in the trees with their legs outstretched. The loose skin between their legs is like a parachute that lets them float from tree to tree.

MARBLED MURRELET

A marbled murrelet sits on her nest in a Douglas-fir tree. These birds spend most of their lives at sea, but they build their nests out of the soft, green moss in the ancient forest's oldest and tallest trees. It takes about 150 years for enough moss to grow in a tree to suit the murrelet.

RACCOON

At the base of the hollow redwood tree where it lives, a raccoon snoops around in search of a snack. Cute as they are, raccoons can really make a racket. They can snarl, hiss, growl, scream, purr, whimper and whinny.

TOTEM POLE

A group of strange faces,
stacked one on top of
another, grins out from
a clearing in the forest.
The Indians of the ancient
forest carved these
giant totem poles out of
whole trees, then painted
them with bright colors.
The faces are of people,
animals or magical spirits.

PACIFIC GIANT SALAMANDER

A Pacific giant salamander
crawls to the edge of
a stream after looking for
bugs beneath the leaves
of a salmonberry bush.
The Pacific giant salamander
lives in cool, moist places
on the forest floor.
It is purplish-brown with
black spots and can grow
to be almost a foot long!

BALD EAGLE

A bald eagle glides over the ancient forest on broad, brown wings. Though the bald eagle is the national symbol of the United States, there are very few left in the wild. Bald eagles are very good at fishing. They soar above winding rivers in search of fish, then swoop down and grab them with their claws.

MARTEN

This intelligent member of the weasel family looks like a cross between a cat and a squirrel. The marten is one of the ancient forest's most curious creatures. Whenever it spies something moving on the forest floor, it scurries down to take a look.

STELLER'S JAY

From the branches of a snag, a Steller's jay makes its noisy call. Steller's jays are easy to recognize by their colorful feathers. Their back and tail feathers are a beautiful, bright blue, but their crown feathers are black.

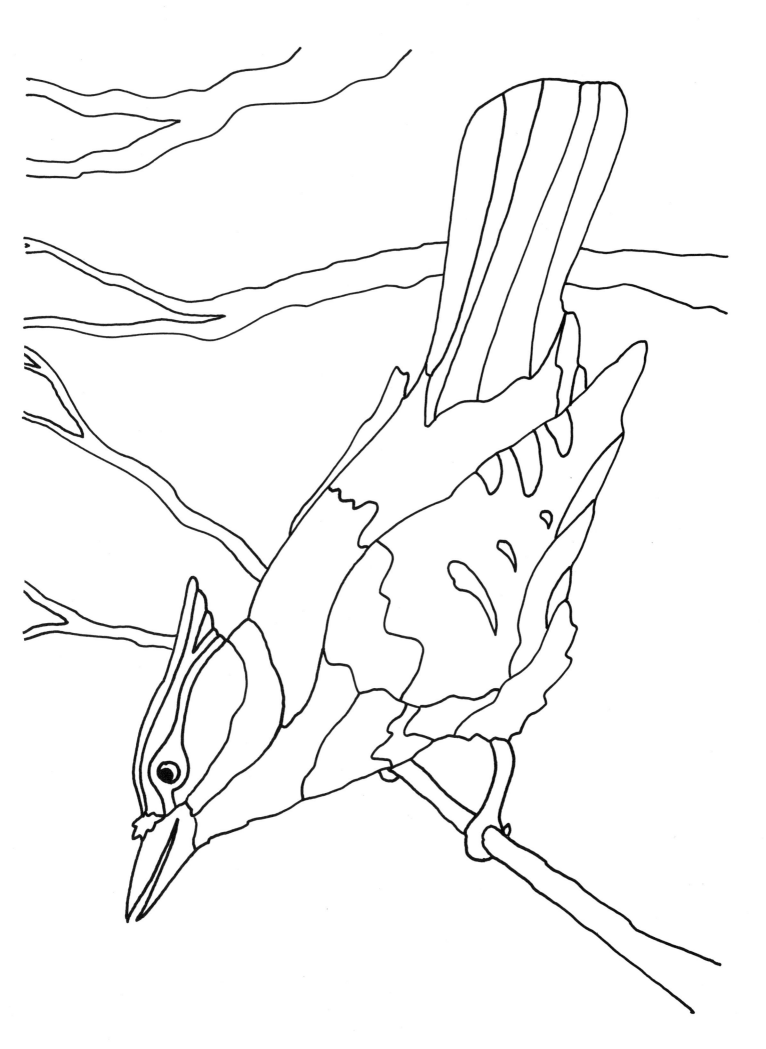

ELK

An elk steps out into a clearing and sniffs the breeze. Like other deer, the elk grows a new set of antlers every year. This elk's antlers are soft and fuzzy because they haven't finished growing. Once they are full grown, the antlers will be hard and spiky.

RED SQUIRREL

A red squirrel peers down from the trunk of a fir tree. Red squirrels aren't as shy as some forest animals. These nosy, noisy creatures jump from branch to branch, chattering loudly all the while. They spend their days gathering acorns and mushrooms and hiding them in secret places.

SOCKEYE SALMON

Deep in the ancient forest, a sockeye salmon charges up a waterfall. After a baby salmon hatches, it swims for many miles down streams and rivers to get to the sea. Years later, when it is time to lay its own eggs, the salmon swims all the way back upstream to return to the place where it was born.

RUFOUS HUMMINGBIRD

With wings buzzing
like propellers on a tiny
helicopter, a rufous
hummingbird hovers
over a group of forest flowers.
Hummingbirds are very
small and fast. Only
when it rests can you
admire the hummingbird's
brightly colored feathers and
needle-thin bill.

The Wilderness Society's Ancient Forest Gifts

All proceeds support The Wilderness Society's campaign to save our ancient forests and other threatened wild lands.

The Wilderness Society Membership. You can become a member of The Wilderness Society with a contribution of $15 or more. Please indicate your membership donation on the order form below.

Color the Ancient Forest. Ages 4–8. 48 pages; $4.95; **Item #102**

Saving Our Ancient Forests.

Learn how you can help save one of our most precious resources. 128 pages; $5.95; **Item #101**

Ancient Forest Tote Bag

Help save our forests by using this colorful and sturdy, full-size tote bag for carrying your groceries. 17″ × 12″ × 5″; $12.95; **Item #103**

Save Our Ancient Forests T-shirt

Display your commitment to our ancient forests with this colorful, 100% premium-cotton T-shirt. Available in small, medium, large and extra-large sizes; $14.95; **Items #104-S, 104-M, 104-L and 104-XL**

The Wild, Wild World of Ancient Forests

28-page teacher's guide and student activity sheet; Grades 4–6; $3.00; **Item #105**

Free with any purchase: **Citizen's Action Kit.** Everything you need to make your voice heard by our lawmakers.

• Cut along dotted line, or photocopy form, fill out and mail along with your check to **The Wilderness Society** •

ORDER FORM

• Please make your check or money order payable to **The Wilderness Society**

• Send to: **The Wilderness Society,** P.O. Box 296, Federalsburg MD 21632-0296

Name: _____

Address: _____

_____

• Please add $3.50 for shipping orders less than $15.00. Add $4.50 for orders of $15.00 or more.

• All Maryland residents add 5% sales tax.

Please allow 6 to 8 weeks for delivery.

QTY.	ITEM #	UNIT PRICE	TOTAL
		Membership	
		Shipping	
		Total	